Little by Little

Music by
Brad Ross

Lyrics by
Ellen Greenfield & Hal Hackady

Story by
Annette Jolles & Ellen Greenfield

SAMUELFRENCH.COM   SAMUELFRENCH.CO.UK

FOR PRODUCTION ENQUIRIES

UNITED STATES AND CANADA
Info@SamuelFrench.com
1-866-598-8449

UNITED KINGDOM AND EUROPE
Plays@SamuelFrench.co.uk
020-7255-4302

Each title is subject to availability from Samuel French, depending upon country of performance. Please be aware that *LITTLE BY LITTLE* may not be licensed by Samuel French in your territory. Professional and amateur producers should contact the nearest Samuel French office or licensing partner to verify availability.

MUSIC USE NOTE

Licensees are solely responsible for obtaining formal written permission from copyright owners to use copyrighted music in the performance of this play and are strongly cautioned to do so. If no such permission is obtained by the licensee, then the licensee must use only original music that the licensee owns and controls. Licensees are solely responsible and liable for all music clearances and shall indemnify the copyright owners of the play(s) and their licensing agent, Samuel French, against any costs, expenses, losses and liabilities arising from the use of music by licensees. Please contact the appropriate music licensing authority in your territory for the rights to any incidental music.

IMPORTANT BILLING AND CREDIT REQUIREMENTS

If you have obtained performance rights to this title, please refer to your licensing agreement for important billing and credit requirements.

LITTLE BY LITTLE opened at The York Theatre Company in New York on January 21, 1999. It was directed by Annette Jolles, with sets by James Morgan, lighting by Mary Jo Dondlinger, costumes by John Carver Sullivan, musical direction by Vincent Trovato, and music and vocal arrangements by Wendy Bobbitt, Joel Fram and Brad Ross.

The cast was as follows:

MAN..............................Darrin Baker
WOMAN I...........................Liz Larsen
WOMAN II.........................Christiane Noll

Originally produced at the Coconut Grove Playhouse, Miami, Florida, Arnold Mittelman, Producing Artistic Director.

PRODUCTION NOTES

LITTLE BY LITTLE is a story told all in song. It is performed with all three actors on stage throughout the show. They step in and out of the action as required, but never leave the stage. An actor who is not involved in a particular scene may either observe the action of the other characters, be present as if in the other characters' minds, or turn his/her back to the action.

There is no literal furniture, scenery, or props. The settings become clear from the actors' words and actions. The playing space therefore needs to provide fluidity and flexibility so that with a single step, the actors are instantly – and believably – in a different location.

When the show starts the characters are in the present day. They are young adults, dressed in contemporary clothing. Over the course of the show, they go back in time, then progress from childhood through adolescence and back into adulthood.

Each actor has a "base" outfit (e.g., a shirt and slacks). Layers of clothing on top of the base and shoe changes (e.g., blazers vs. sweatshirts; high heels vs. sneakers) indicate the stages of their lives.

MUSICAL NUMBERS

Opening / Friendship and Love	ALL
Friendship and Love (Coda)	ALL
Homework	ALL
Tag	ALL
Homework (Reprise)	ALL
Little by Little I	ALL
Life and All That	ALL
Starlight	ALL
Popcorn	MAN and WOMAN 1
Just Between Us	ALL
I'm Not	WOMAN 2
Little by Little II	ALL
A Little Hustle	ALL
Bouquet Time	ALL
Rainbows	MAN and WOMAN 1
Rainbows (Coda)	WOMAN 1
Nocturne	WOMAN 1
Little by Little III	ALL
Yes	ALL
Nocturne (Reprise)	WOMAN 1
The Schmooze	MAN and WOMAN 2
Take the World Away	WOMAN 2
Homework (Reprise II)	MAN and WOMAN 2
Okay	MAN
If You Only Knew	ALL
Little by Little IV	ALL
Yes (Reprise)	WOMAN 1 and MAN
If You Loved Me	ALL
I'm Not (Reprise)	WOMAN 2
Tell Me	MAN
I Ought to Cry	WOMAN 1
Little by Little V	ALL
So It Goes	ALL
Popcorn II	ALL
I'm a Rotten Person	ALL
Starlight (Reprise)	ALL
A Journey That Never Ends	ALL

CHARACTERS

All three characters are in their early 20s to early 30s. They've been best friends since childhood.

WOMAN 1: Charismatic and attractive. The type of woman who, although bright and competent, tends to rely on her sex appeal to get what she wants. She has a tendency to be self-centered and impulsive.

WOMAN 2: While also physically appealing, WOMAN 2 is more confident of her abilities than her appearance. As WOMAN 1's best friend, she sees herself as smart and reliable, not desirable. She's accommodating to a fault.

MAN: The most unsophisticated of the three — trusting, good-natured, not given to introspection. He's cute, charming, loyal, optimistic — a genuinely nice guy who believes that dreams really can come true.

OPENING / FRIENDSHIP AND LOVE

*(Lights come up to reveal WOMAN 1, MAN and WOMAN 2. They
    sing...)*

W1.
LITTLE BY LITTLE...
   W2.
LITTLE BY LITTLE...
   ALL.
LITTLE BY LITTLE...

*(Lights and music change. They look at one another, then turn and
    sing to the audience...)*

   ALL.
BEFORE WE GET STARTED, A COMMENT OR TWO
IF, AS WE UNFOLD OUR TALE,
IT SEEMS FAMILIAR TO YOU
THAT WOULDN'T SURPRISE US
THE TRUTH OF IT IS
OUR STORY COULD EASILY BE YOURS,
   MAN.
BE HERS
   W1.
OR BE HIS

   MAN.
AND SO BECAUSE NO ONE HERE IS BLAMELESS
   W1.
WE FIGURE IT'S BEST THAT WE GO NAMELESS
   W2.
SO YOU CAN RELAX
AS WE PRESENT OUR VERSION OF
   ALL.
THE TROUBLES THAT COME OF MIXING
FRIENDSHIP AND LOVE
TAKE US, FOR EXAMPLE,
A CLASSICAL CASE,
A TRIO OF FRIENDS,
THE LIFELONG FRIENDS YOU NEVER REPLACE

MAN.
THINGS USED TO BE SIMPLE
W1/W2.
THEY GOT SO COMPLEX
ALL.
WE THOUGHT WE WOULD ALWAYS BE BEST FRIENDS
MAN.
AND THEN THERE WAS
ALL.
SEX!

ALL.
WE NEED TO GO BACK TO ADOLESCENCE,
RELIVE THE BEGINNING OF PUBESCENCE
W1.
EXAMINE OUR ACTIONS
MAN.
AND THE CONSEQUENCES OF
ALL.
TO CLEAR UP THE MESS WE MADE OF
FRIENDSHIP AND LOVE

(They begin to get caught up in their story, forgetting the audience as the tension builds.)

MAN.
WHEN LOVE ERUPTS
OUR NERVES DO TEND TO GET JANGLED
W2.
MISTAKES ARE MADE
W1.
AND THINGS ARE SAID WE DON'T MEAN
ALL.
OUR FEARS, OUR HOPES, OUR HEARTS
CAN GET SO ENTANGLED AND MANGLED
THAT FRIENDSHIP GETS MASHED IN BETWEEN

(They become aware of the audience again.)

ALL.
BEFORE WE GO ONWARD
WE'VE GOT TO GO BACK
TO TRY TO DISCOVER HOW
WE GOT SO FAR OFF THE TRACK

(As they realize they need to revisit what happened in the past, they begin to trade the outer pieces of their adult clothing for the garments of their younger days.)

MAN.
AND AS WE REVISIT EACH DECISION
    W1.
WE MADE WITH OUR HORMONE-TINTED VISION
    W2.
CONSIDER OUR STORY AS THE TRUE ADVENTURES OF
    W1.
THREE TYPICAL PEOPLE WHO ARE,
    MAN.
MUCH LIKE YOU ARE,
    W2.
ALTERED THROUGH OUR
    ALL.
FRIENDSHIP
    W1.
FRIENDSHIP
    MAN.
FRIENDSHIP
    ALL.
AND LOVE

FRIENDSHIP AND LOVE CODA

    ALL.
WE THOUGHT WE WOULD ALWAYS BE
BEST FRIENDS...
BEST FRIENDS...

(They complete the change from adult clothing into kids' clothing. As they do, it begins to thunder and rain.)

HOMEWORK

(The three go back in time. They are now in early adolescence. They lie in a clump, draped over one another innocently, waiting out the storm.)

    W1.
I'M BORED

MAN.
ME TOO
   W2.
ME THREE

   W1.
I'M BORED
   W2.
WE KNOW
   MAN.
I'M MAD!

   MAN.
THAT HOMEWORK IS THE WORST I'VE EVER SEEN
THAT PROBLEM WITH THE STUPID TRAIN
   W1.
IT'S NOT THE TRAIN THAT'S STUPID
   W2.
DON'T BE MEAN!
   W1.
I'M SICK OF ALL THIS STUPID RAIN!

   W2.
IT'S STOPPING
   W1.
LET'S MOTOR!
   MAN.
HEY, LOOK THERE— A RAINBOW!
   W2.
IT'S GORGEOUS, IT'S LIKE...
   MAN.
A REWARD!

   W1/W2. What?

   MAN.
LIKE, "THANKS FOR YOUR PATIENCE"
   W2.
A THANK YOU FROM HEAVEN,
THAT'S COSMIC!
   W1.
OH, GAG ME!
I'M BORED!

TAG

(W1 "tags" W2 and runs away.)

W1.
YOU'RE IT
W2.
YOU'RE IT

(W2 tags MAN and gloats. He sits there, feigning a pout.)

W2.
I GOTCHA, HA
YOU CAN'T CATCH ME
YOU CAN'T CATCH ME!
YOU'RE IT!

(W2 moves close to MAN trying to make him play. He fakes her out, tags her and runs away. They all chase one another.)

MAN.
YOU'RE IT!
I GOTCHA, HA!
YOU CAN'T CATCH ME!
YOU CAN'T TOUCH ME!

MAN/W1.
JUST TRY TO CATCH ME
TRY TO TOUCH ME
HA-HA-HA

W2.
YOU'RE IT
(W2 catches W1.) YOU'RE IT
W1.
YOU'RE IT

(W1 grabs MAN; they freeze as we hear his thoughts.)

MAN.
WHAT DO I FEEL?
WHAT'S GOING ON?
SOMETHING IS REALLY — WOW!

WHAT DID SHE DO?

MAN. *(Continued)*
WHAT DOES SHE KNOW?
WHAT IF SHE SEES?
WHAT IF I SHOW HER?

WHAT DID I SAY?
WHAT SHOULD I DO?
OOH, WHAT'S IT DOING NOW?

OUT OF CONTROL!
OUT OF MY HANDS
TOTALLY CAUGHT OFF GUARD

IF I CAN BE SO EASILY STIRRED,
THEN ALL THE RULES ARE SUDDENLY BLURRED
IT'S HARD TO THINK WHEN THIS HAS OCCURRED
OH, HARD IS THE WORD
IT'S HARD!

(They resume the game. MAN is still "it.")

   W1.
YOU CAN'T CATCH ME
   W2.
YOU CAN'T TOUCH ME
   W1.
JUST TRY TO CATCH ME
   W2.
TRY TO TOUCH ME
   W1/W2.
HA HA HA
   MAN.
YOU'RE IT!

(MAN tags W1; they freeze as we hear her thoughts.)

   W1.
WHAT A CURIOUS RUSH I'M FEELING, A
KIND OF BUZZ ON MY SKIN
DOESN'T FEEL LIKE A CRUSH, IT'S DIFFERENT, IT'S
MAYBE EVEN A SIN!

HOW EXCITING, HOW TRULY AWESOME, I
NEVER PLAYED SUCH A GAME
SOMETHING TOTALLY NEW JUST HAPPENED, I

W1. *(Continued)*
HOPE HE KNOWS IT, I
HOPE HE'S FEELING THE SAME

WILD AND WOBBLY, AND OOH, I LIKE IT, I
MAYBE SHOULDN'T, BUT THEN
IF HE'S FEELING IT TOO,
CAN'T HELP IT, I
HOPE HE IS AND I
HOPE HE DOES IT AGAIN!

(The game resumes. W1 is "it.")

   MAN/W2.
TAG
   W1.
(W1 tags MAN) YOU'RE IT
   MAN.
(MAN tags W2) YOU'RE IT

(They freeze as we hear W2's thoughts.)

   W2.
OH, MY GOD!
OH, NO! OH, NO!
I THINK I BETTER GO
I THINK I WANT TO STAY
I KNOW I OUGHT TO GO
BUT,

OH, MY GOD!
IT'S WEIRD, SO WEIRD
I THINK IT'S WHAT I'VE FEARED
I THINK IT'S WHAT I'VE HEARD ABOUT
THIS LOVE STUFF

I AM UNPREPARED
AND I'M REALLY SCARED, I MEAN IT!
GOTTA STAY REAL CALM
GOD, I WANT MY MOM, I MEAN IT!

BUT DESPITE MY FEAR
I AM ROOTED HERE
THOUGH I KNOW I OUGHT TO RUN
BEING SCARED LIKE THIS IS FUN

W2. *(Continued)*
OH, MY GOD
OH, NO! OH, NO!
MY FACE IS BURNING HOT
COULD I BE GETTING SICK?
I DON'T KNOW WHAT I'VE GOT
BUT, OH
CAN'T MOVE...
DON'T MOVE...
DON'T MOVE...

(The game resumes. W2 is "it.")

  ALL. *(Overlapping).*
TAG
YOU'RE IT
I GOTCHA, HA
YOU CAN'T CATCH ME
YOU CAN'T CATCH ME
YOU CAN'T CATCH ME
CATCH ME
TOUCH/CATCH ME
TAG/TOUCH ME
DARE YOU
CATCH ME
DARE YOU
TOUCH ME
DARE YOU
GOTCHA, HA
I GOTCHA, HA

  W2.
(W2 tags MAN) YOU'RE IT
  MAN.
(MAN tags both girls) YOU'RE IT

  W1/W2.
YOU'RE IT

*(Both girls tag MAN and hold onto him in a sexually-charged clump,
    with MAN in the middle. They remain in that pose through the
    end of the song. Their words belie their feelings.)*

  MAN.
I'M BORED

W2.
ME TOO
W1.
ME THREE

W1/W2.
I'M BORED
MAN.
BORED STIFF!

HOMEWORK (Reprise)

(MAN squirms out of the clump.)

MAN.
WELL, ALGEBRA TO DO,
I BETTER GO
W1.
CAN'T YOU DO IT LATER?
W2.
NO!
BETTER GET IT OVER
MAN.
YEAH, GUESS SO
I WISH I COULD TELL AN X FROM A Y
W1.
I'LL HELP YOU
MAN.
YOU WILL?
W2.
NO! HE HAS TO TRY
W1.
HE DOES?
W2. Uh-huh...
'BYE!
W1.
'BYE...
MAN.'
BYE...

(MAN "exits," moving into his own space. W2 approaches W1 as if to talk, but W1 turns away, caught up in her new feelings. W2 walks away. They remain separate as they sing...)

LITTLE BY LITTLE I

W2.
LITTLE BY LITTLE
WE OPEN THE DOOR
FIRST JUST A CRACK
   W1/W2.
THEN A LITTLE BIT MORE
   ALL.
WIDER AND WIDER
THAN EVER BEFORE
LEARNING HOW MUCH WE DON'T KNOW
LITTLE BY LITTLE
WE GROW

(During a musical transition, the actors change their outer garments to indicate the passage of time. They are now in their mid-teens.)

(Once changed, there is a pantomime in which W1 flirts with MAN. He revels in her attention, as W2 observes. W1 and W2 coyly giggle and confer. He preens and struts, showing off for them. Encouraged by W1, W2 imitates his swaggering walk and both girls have a good laugh at his expense. He turns away, embarrassed and deflated.)

(The two girls converse...)

LIFE AND ALL THAT

W2.
HAVE YOU NOTICED ANYTHING
STRANGE ABOUT HIM?
   W1.
SOMETHING STRANGE?
HE'S ALWAYS STRANGE
   W2.
I KNOW, BUT SOMETHING NEW

IN HIS EYES, HIS MANNER, A
CHANGE ABOUT HIM
   W1.
MORE MATURE?
I'M NOT SO SURE
BUT TALLER, CUTER TOO

W2.
REALLY?
W1.
REALLY!
W2.
REALLY

(As the girls contemplate one another's responses, MAN – in a separate space – expresses his own thoughts.)

MAN.
X MINUS Y
COULD EQUAL THREE MINUS ONE AND THAT LEAVES TWO
BUT IF THAT IS TRUE
I MUST CHOOSE ONE
BUT THEN IF I DO
I COULD LOSE ONE

(The girls continue their conversation.)

W2.
DO YOU EVER THINK ABOUT
LIFE AND ALL THAT?
WHY WE'RE BORN
AND ARE WE BORN
WITH ALL OUR FUTURE PLANNED?

W1.
LIKE, PREDESTINED HUSBAND AND
WIFE AND ALL THAT?
W2.
MAYBE
W1.
REALLY?
W2.
MAYBE

W1.	**MAN.**
I CAN'T BELIEVE IT'S TRUE	IT ISN'T FAIR
THAT THERE'S, LIKE, A	
MASTER LIST	
I THINK IT'S UP TO YOU,	WHAT SHOULD I DO?
THE REASON THAT	
YOU EXIST	

W2.
WHAT ABOUT LOVE?
  W1.
WHAT DO YOU MEAN?
  W2.
DON'T YOU BELIEVE IN FATE?   **MAN.**
                                        X EQUALS WHO?

ONE REAL LOVE,
ONE TRUE MATE
  W1.
I'D BE THRILLED WITH ONE REAL DATE!

  ALL.
IT'S A GREAT, BIG QUESTION MARK
LIFE AND ALL THAT
WHAT, WHY, WHEN, WHO
HOW TO FIND THE KEY
HOW TO ACE THE TEST THAT IS LIFE
HOW TO CHOOSE THE BEST ABOUT LIFE
  W1.
ABOUT BOYS AND ALL THAT
  MAN.
GIRLS AND ALL THAT
  W2.
LOVE AND ALL THAT
  ALL.
LIFE AND ALL THAT
AND ALL THAT LIFE CAN BE

STARLIGHT

(As a tremolo is heard, the three look up. Each makes a wish on the first evening star.)

  ALL.
STARLIGHT
STARBRIGHT
FIRST STAR I SEE TONIGHT

(MAN looks at W1 and then W2, as if trying to choose between them.)

  W1/W2.
STARLIGHT
STARBRIGHT

W1/W2. *(Continued)*
FIRST STAR I SEE TONIGHT
   MAN.
WISH I MAY

(W2 sneaks a peek at MAN. He takes a step toward her. She turns away, thrilled but needing a moment to collect herself.)

   W2.
WISH I MIGHT

(MAN feels rejected and turns to W1 who is clearly receptive. W2 turns to MAN again, but he is now moving toward W1. Having missed her chance, W2 is disappointed)

   W1/W2.
HAVE THIS WISH I WISH
   W1.
I WISH *(W1 extends her hand to MAN; he takes it)*
TONIGHT

   W2.
STARLIGHT
STARBRIGHT
TONIGHT

(W2 retreats)

POPCORN

(MAN and W1 go on a date to the movies. They sit facing upstage, as if looking at the movie screen. He turns and faces the audience. As he mimes eating popcorn, he wonders...)

   MAN.
WHAT WOULD HAPPEN IF I ACCIDENTALLY,
UNINTENTIONALLY TOUCH HER BREAST?
AS I'M PASSING HER THE POPCORN
WHAT'S THE BEST SCENARIO?

(At various moments, under the pretense of passing popcorn, he "feels her up.")

WOULD SHE WORRY THAT I'D THINK SHE'S PARANOID
IF SHE ASKED ME TO REMOVE MY HAND?

MAN. *(Continued)*
LIKE IT WASN'T THERE BY ACCIDENT,
BUT PLANNED

OR SHE COULD
SMILE AND HAVE SOME POPCORN
LIKE SHE'S UNAWARE
AS I HOLD THE POPCORN
I'M TOUCHING HER THERE

WHAT WOULD HAPPEN, WHAT'S THE WORST SCENARIO?
WOULD SHE SCREAM AND SLAP MY FACE?
I'D BE ASKED TO LEAVE THE THEATER IN DISGRACE
MAYBE CHARGED WITH LEWD BEHAVIOR
END UP IN A PRISON CELL
IT COULD REALLY BE MY BUTT!
BUT, WHAT THE HELL

(He turns back upstage, she turns downstage. Throughout the rest of the song, his action with the popcorn continues.)

W1.
WHAT WOULD HAPPEN IF I LET HIS HAND REMAIN?
WOULD HE THINK THAT I'M AN EASY MAKE?
ON THE OTHER HAND IF I SHOULD WHISPER
"TAKE YOUR HAND AWAY"
WOULD HE THINK I'M BEING SLIGHTLY PARANOID,
THINKING THAT HE'S TRY'N'A COP A FEEL?
WHEN HE'S ONLY PASSING POPCORN
GIRL, GET REAL!

I COULD CRY
SEXUAL HARASSMENT
BUT IT'S HARD TO PROVE
SEXUAL HARASSMENT
DID HIS HAND JUST MOVE?

WHAT IS HAPPENING IS NOT BY ACCIDENT
I COULD EITHER HOLLER "STOP!"
OR KEEP WAITING FOR THE OTHER HAND TO DROP

I'LL CONTINUE EATING POPCORN
WHILE I LET HIM HUNT AND PECK
SO HE'LL THINK THAT I'M A SLUT
BUT WHAT THE HECK!

(MAN turns back downstage. They both stay facing the audience until the end of the number.)

BOTH.
OH, NO, WE'VE
EATEN ALL THE POPCORN
W1.
MONUMENTAL DRAG!
BOTH.
IT WAS REALLY STUPID
TO FINISH THE BAG

MAN.
WHAT WOULD HAPPEN IF I JUST KEEP PASSING IT?
W1.
WHAT'S HE THINKING, WOULD HE DARE?
MAN.
IF I PASS IT, WILL SHE TAKE IT?
W1.
PUT IT THERE!

BOTH.
IT'LL HAPPEN IF IT HAPPENS
AND WE'LL JUST GO ON AND ON
EATING NONEXISTENT POPCORN
TILL IT'S GONE!

JUST BETWEEN US

(MAN and W1 kiss; W2 observes.)

W2.
OH, MY GOD!
OH, NO
OH, NO

OH, PLEASE DON'T LET THIS BE
I ALWAYS DREAMED THAT HE
WOULD FALL IN LOVE WITH ME

OH, NO...

(W1 and MAN both approach W2; she's caught in the middle. It is as though W1 and MAN are each having separate conversations

*with W2; they don't hear one another, but W2 hears both of
them.)*

W1.
WAIT'LL YOU HEAR
I'M DYING TO TELL YOU
BUT PROMISE,
IT'S JUST BETWEEN US

                                     W2.
                                       I PROMISE
                                       IT'S JUST BETWEEN US

     MAN.
WAIT'LL YOU HEAR!
WHAT I HAVE TO TELL YOU
BUT PROMISE,
IT'S JUST BETWEEN US

                                       I PROMISE,
                                       IT'S JUST BETWEEN US

     W1.
HE IS IN LOVE WITH ME
     MAN.
SHE IS THE ONE!
     W1.
IT'S SO COOL!
     MAN.
SHE'S SO...
     BOTH.
COOL, BUT LIKE FIRE!

                                       W2.
                                       THAT'S TERRIFIC!

     BOTH.
YEAH,
     W1.
BUT BEING HIS LOVE
THAT'S INTENSE, AM I READY?
     MAN.
I WANT TO GO STEADY
     BOTH.
SHOULD I GO AHEAD?
     W1.
EVEN THOUGH
SAYING NO
     BOTH.
COULD BE DIRE!
YOU GOTTA HELP ME

                                       W2.
                                       WHAT?

BOTH.
YOU COULD FIND OUT
WHAT HE/SHE'S REALLY THINKING
BUT KEEPING IT JUST BETWEEN US

          W2.
          NO, I COULDN'T
          NO, I WON'T

YOU COULD FIND OUT
OH, PLEASE, BE MY BUDDY
YOU HAVE TO, IT'S JUST BETWEEN,
I MEAN IT, REALLY
JUST BETWEEN...
YOU COULD FIND OUT

          NO

IT'S EASY FOR YOU,

          NO

YOU MUST
DON'T YOU TRUST ME?
I PROMISE IT'S JUST BETWEEN US!

          OH, MY GOD,
          WELL, JUST THIS ONCE!

YES!

(Musical transition. Time passage. W1 and MAN flirt as W2 observes in exasperation. They both corner W2 again.)

BOTH.
WHAT DID HE/SHE SAY?

          W2.
          OH,
          MY GOODNESS

DON'T LEAVE OUT A COMMA
DON'T WORRY,
IT'S JUST BETWEEN US

          I DON'T KNOW WHAT I
          OUGHT TO DO

WHAT DID HE/SHE SAY?

          OH,
          MY GOODNESS

DON'T BUILD UP THE DRAMA
JUST HURRY,
IT'S JUST BETWEEN US!

          I COULD RUIN THIS
          FOR YOU

TELL ME THE TRUTH
IS HE/SHE REALLY IN LOVE?

W2. (*Continued*)
I COULD
MAKE UP A LIE
AND YOU'D BUY IT!
IMAGINE THAT!

BOTH. (*Continued*)
TO TELL YOU THE TRUTH
I'M AFRAID OF REJECTION

AND STEAL HIS
AFFECTION

BUT YOU'RE MY PROTECTION

BUT NO!
I'M TOO CHICKEN
TO TRY IT!

YOU GOTTA HELP ME
TELL ME THE TRUTH

OH,
MY GOODNESS!

PLEASE STOP THE SUSPENSE, IT'S
A PROMISE,
IT'S JUST BETWEEN US

I COULD NEVER
TELL A LIE

TELL ME THE TRUTH

I HATE THIS!

IT'S BAD, I CAN SENSE, IT'S
THERE'S NOTHING
AT ALL BETWEEN US,
HE/SHE DOESN'T LOVE ME AT ALL

I'LL
TELL YOU THE TRUTH
NO NEED FOR
DEJECTION

MAN.
THE LIGHT IS A GREEN ONE?
W1.
HE SAID I'M BEWITCHING?

IF EVER I'VE SEEN ONE!

WHILE PANTING AND
TWITCHING

BOTH.
HONEST, YOU SWEAR TO GOD?

SWEAR TO GOD
AND HOPE TO PERISH

THANK YOU
THANK YOU
PLEASE, KEEP THIS
ALL.
JUST BETWEEN US!

(W1 and MAN go off together; W2 is left alone.)

I'M NOT

W2.
OH, MY GOD!
OH, NO...

HE IS
WELL, TO ME, HE'S SIMPLY GREAT
AND SHE IS,
WELL, TO HIM, THE PERFECT DATE

I'M NOT
NOT AS SPICY, NOT AS HOT
I'M NOT
I'M NICE, WHICH SIGNALS BLAND
SO, IN DEMAND
I'M NOT

HE IS
HE'S EXCEPTIONALLY CUTE
AND SHE IS
WELL, HIS FIRST FORBIDDEN FRUIT
I'M NOT
NOT AS RIPE, I'M NOT HIS TYPE
I'M NOT
NO, I'M TOO NICE, TOO SMART
THE GIRL TO WIN HIS HEART
I'M NOT

I'M DOOMED TO BE THEIR PAL, I SEE MY FATE NOW
MY FOOLISH DREAMS OF HIM, I'LL PUT AWAY
SUCCESS WILL BE MY GOAL AND I CAN'T WAIT NOW
TO HEAR HOW THEY'LL SAY

"OH, MY GOD,
WE KNEW HER WHEN"
AS EVERY PLAN I PLAN COMES TRUE
I'LL ALWAYS BE SO GRACIOUS TO
THE LITTLE PEOPLE I ONCE KNEW

'CAUSE HE IS
WELL, THE BOY THAT I'LL RECALL

W2. *(Continued)*
AND SHE IS
WELL, THE GIRL WHO HAS IT ALL
I'M NOT
WELL, NOT YET, BUT WAIT AND SEE

I'M NOT AS FORMED AS SOME, BUT
I'M NOT WHAT I'LL BECOME AND
BELIEVE ME
THEY'LL SOON SEE
EXACTLY WHAT I'VE GOT
INSTEAD OF WHAT
I'M NOT!

LITTLE BY LITTLE II

MAN.
LITTLE BY LITTLE WE GROW
W2.
LITTLE BY LITTLE WE GROW
W1.
LITTLE BY LITTLE WE GROW
ALL.
LITTLE BY LITTLE WE GROW

(They begin to change clothing, transforming from teenagers to young, professional adults.)

ALL.
PICK OUT A STAR THAT YOU'LL FOLLOW FROM HERE
NERVOUS, EXCITED AND NOT WITHOUT FEAR
ENTER A WORLD THAT YOU'LL STAND ON ITS EAR
TAKING EACH DAY BY SURPRISE
TIME TO TRY LIFE ON FOR SIZE

(During a musical transition, they complete the costume change. In the next song, they share and celebrate their sense of independence and budding success.)

A LITTLE HUSTLE

ALL.
A LITTLE HUSTLE, PLUS
A LITTLE MUSCLE, PLUS
A LITTLE PREP,

ALL. *(Continued)*
A LITTLE LUCK,
A LOTTA GRIT
THE PROPER PLATITUDE,
A WINNING ATTITUDE,
A MACHO HANDSHAKE
AND A MODICUM OF WIT

W1.
WHEN YOU BECOME AN EMPLOYEE
IF YOU'RE AT ALL AMBITIOUS
DON'T BE A DULL, LITTLE WORKER BEE
YOU WON'T GO FAR

LOOK LIKE A WINNER, THAT'S THE KEY
TARGET THE SOURCE OF POWER
MAKE AN IMPRESSION AND ONE-TWO-THREE
A RISING STAR
IS WHO YOU ARE

ALL.
A LITTLE HUSTLE, PLUS
A LITTLE MUSCLE, PLUS
W1.
A LITTLE SMILE
A LITTLE SMARTS
A LOTTA NERVE

ALL.
THE PROPER PLATITUDE,
A WINNING ATTITUDE,
W1.
DESIGNER CLOTHING
CUT TO CLING TO EVERY CURVE

W2.
WORK IS A SOURCE OF ENDLESS KICKS
WORK IS WHERE I'M INSPIRED
ENERGY FLOWS, COGITATION CLICKS
AT CYBER-SPEED

STAY ABOVE OFFICE POLITICS
MASTER THE SKILLS THAT MATTER
BUSINESS TO WIN OR A GLITCH TO FIX
IT'S ME THEY NEED
'CAUSE I SUCCEED

ALL.
A LITTLE HUSTLE, PLUS
A LITTLE MUSCLE, PLUS
   W2.
A LITTLE DRIVE
A LITTLE SWEAT
A LOTTA GRACE

   ALL.
THE PROPER PLATITUDE,
A WINNING ATTITUDE,
   W2.
AN ERGONOMIC CHAIR
AND CARPAL TUNNEL BRACE

   MAN.
I'M REMARKABLY LUCKY THAT
I'M THE AFFABLE KIND
I'M INCREDIBLY SKILLFUL AT
UNLOCKING A FASTENED MIND

I AM ON THE ASCENDANT
SKYWARD BOUND, WHAT A TIME!
EXCITING DEALS TO CLOSE (*He looks at W1*)
A GIRL SO HOT, SHE GLOWS
I MEAN, MY SLICE OF LIFE IS PRIME

   ALL.
A LITTLE HUSTLE, PLUS
A LITTLE MUSCLE, PLUS
   MAN.
A LITTLE CHAT
A LITTLE STYLE
A LOTTA CHARM

   ALL.
THE PROPER PLATITUDE,
A WINNING ATTITUDE,
   MAN.
INNATE CHARISMA AND
A LOOKER ON YOUR ARM

   ALL.
A LITTLE HUSTLE, PLUS
A LITTLE MUSCLE, PLUS

ALL. *(Continued)*
A LITTLE PREP
A LITTLE LUCK
A LOTTA GRIT

THE PROPER PLATITUDE,
A WINNING ATTITUDE,
   W2.
AMAZING SKILL
   MAN.
THAT YOU CAN BILL FOR
   W1.
AND A ROLODEX TO KILL FOR
    ALL.
AND A MODICUM
OF WIT!

BOUQUET TIME

(All three attend a wedding. They watch the wedding procession file in – and very quickly – out.)

   W2.
CATCH-THE-BOUQUET-TIME!
   W1.
CORNBALL!

(MAN encourages W1 to catch the bouquet)

   MAN.
DON'T BE A CYNIC,
CATCH THE BOUQUET
RIGHT HERE
OVER HERE,
OVER HERE,
OVER HEEEEERE!

(The women intentionally miss the bouquet. It falls to the floor. MAN and W1 begin to dance. W2 looks lost and W1 encourages MAN to dance with her. As he does, he whispers something in her ear, then turns back to W1. Trying to hide her feelings, W2 abruptly leaves as MAN takes W1 in his arms and they resume dancing. He begins to sing...)

RAINBOWS

MAN.
I LOOKED AT THE BRIDE WHEN SHE SAID, "I DO"
AND FANTASIZED THAT SHE WAS YOU
AND HE WAS ME AND WE WERE BEING MARRIED
   W1.
WEDDINGS ARE HIGHLY CONTAGIOUS
   MAN.
I'M THINKIN' DIAMOND RINGS
   W1.
COMING TO ONE WAS COURAGEOUS
   MAN.
AND HONEYMOON HOTELS
I'M HEARIN' WEDDING BELLS
I'VE STARTED SEEIN' THINGS

I'M SEEIN' RAINBOWS
ALL OVER THE PLACE
AS MANY RAINBOWS
AS YOU CAN CHASE
I'M SEEIN' SUNSHINE AHEAD
ALL YOU CAN SPREAD
I SEE A BIG DOUBLE BED OF ROSES FOR YOU AND ME

DON'T INTERRUPT
HUSH UP AND LISTEN
WHY PUT US ON HOLD?
WE'RE RISKIN' MISSIN' OUR POT OF GOLD

LET'S MARRY NOW, PRESENT TENSE
WHY PAY TWO RENTS?
UNNECESSARY EXPENSE
AM I MAKIN' SENSE OR WHAT?

I SEE US HAPPY EVER AFTER
A FAIRYTALE LIFE OF LOVE 'N LAUGHTER
AS MAN AND WIFE
A NORMAN ROCKWELL CLICHÉ
KIDS RIGHT AWAY
I SEE ME WATCHIN' THE WAY YOU PLAY WITH THEM
LET'S HAVE THREE!

TWO BOYS, A GIRL AND ONE DALMATIAN
THE WHOLE BALL OF WAX

MAN. *(Continued)*
JOINT DECLARATION!
LESS INCOME TAX
I'M TALKIN' LIFE A LA MODE
JUST DOWN THE ROAD
SKIES ARE UNLOADIN'
A LOAD OF RAINBOWS FOR YOU AND ME

I'M TALKIN' TURKEY FOR THANKSGIVIN'
AND ALL YOU CAN EAT
I'M TALKIN' LIVIN' ON EASY STREET
I'M TALKIN' BIG TIME HELLO
CHAMPAGNE TO GO
AND TALK ABOUT ROLLIN' IN DOUGH
IT'S GONNA BE — BOY, OH, BOY!

KNOCK ONCE FOR "YES" IF I HAVE SOLD YA
AM I GETTIN' THROUGH?
OH, HAVE I TOLD YA THAT I LOVE YOU
I'M SEEIN' RAINBOWS TO DIE
A LIFETIME SUPPLY
I MEAN AS FAR AS THE EYE CAN SEE
WITH A SKY MARQUEE
READIN' RAINBOWS FREE
I'LL BE GUARANTEEIN' THEM
FROM NOW ON!

*(Instead of answering him, she stops him with a kiss and leads him to
    bed.)*

RAINBOWS CODA

W1.
... ALL YOU CAN SPREAD
I SEE A BIG DOUBLE BED...

(They make love; he falls asleep. As he sleeps, she ponders...)

NOCTURNE

W1.
HOW ABOUT THAT? A REAL PROPOSAL, WITH
LOVE AND RAINBOWS AND ALL
QUITE A TEMPTING APPEAL,

W1. *(Continued)*
SO WHY DID I
DODGE, DISTRACT HIM, AND STALL?

LOOK AT MY SWEET MISTER HAPPINESS
SO BLISSFUL, EACH SNORE IS A PURR
DREAMING A LIFETIME OF RAPTURE
SO CONTENT, SO SECURE, SO CERTAIN

LOOK HOW HIS FACE IS ALL MASHED, TRY NOT TO
LOOK AT THAT DRIBBLE OF DROOL
LOOK AT ME BRIMMING WITH PASSION
WHEN HE LOOKS LIKE SUCH A FOOL

IT'S LOVE,
MUST BE LOVE, THIS
FILTER ON MY EYES
VEILING LITTLE FAULTS AND FLAWS,
TO LOVE
IS TO LOVE, IT'S
NOT TO ANALYZE,
ANALYSIS MIGHT GIVE ME PAUSE...

IT ISN'T THAT I DON'T BELIEVE HE'S CAPABLE OF RAINBOWS
ISN'T THAT I THINK HE WON'T SUCCEED
NO, IT
ISN'T THAT AT ALL; IT'S, WELL, THEY'RE <u>HIS</u> DAMN RAINBOWS
HAS HE EVEN WONDERED IF IT'S RAINBOWS THAT I NEED?

I MEAN, IT ISN'T THAT I MIGHT NOT ADORE THEM
AND IT ISN'T THAT HE ISN'T
FOR ME

IT'S ONLY THAT, FOR NOW
I MEAN, HOW DO I KNOW
WHO I'LL WANT
NO, I MEAN, WHO I'LL BE
NO, I MEAN, WHAT I'LL WANT
WHAT I MEAN IS,
I WANT TO WAIT AND SEE

IT ISN'T UP TO HIM TO MAP OUT MY FUTURE
IT ISN'T HIS JOB
ISN'T THAT FOR ME TO CHOOSE?
IT ISN'T THAT I CAN'T, I CAN

W1. *(Continued)*
I WILL, REAL SOON, BUT LOOK,
RIGHT NOW
ISN'T HE SOMETHING FINE?
AREN'T WE HAVING FUN?

AND OH...

OH, THE DREAMS HE CAN WEAVE, HIS RAINBOWS ARE
SUCH A COMFORTING SIGHT
MAKES ME WANT TO BELIEVE THAT RAINBOWS ARE
MORE THAN WATER AND LIGHT

JUST
LOOK AT MY SWEET MISTER HAPPINESS
SO CERTAIN HE KNOWS WHAT I'LL CHOOSE
LOOK AT THAT FACE, WHAT A SNAPSHOT, I'D BE
HEARTSICK IF I SHOULD LOSE HIM

WHAT HOLDS ME BACK, AM I CRAZY? NO ONE
ELSE COULD BE LOVING AS HE
I COULD BE FILLED WITH ELATION, IF I
ONLY KNEW HIS RAINBOWS
WOULD BE ENOUGH FOR ME

(She snuggles against him, as if settling in for the night.)

LITTLE BY LITTLE III

(W2 enters and exchanges a look with W1. All three move into their own spaces.)

   W2.
CHOICES WERE EASY WHEN CRAYONS WERE GREEN
   W1.
GREEN AND
   W2/W1.
RED, BLUE, AND YELLOW AND NOTHING BETWEEN
   ALL.
TURQUOISE AND FUCHSIA AND AQUAMARINE
MAKE IT MUCH HARDER TO CHOOSE
WHICH OF LIFE'S COLORS TO USE

YES

(W2 sits, as if at her desk at work.)

W2.
LOOK AT THIS GRAPH
THIS CAN'T BE RIGHT
SHOULD HAVE STAYED LATE
TO REVIEW THIS LAST NIGHT
FIND THE MISTAKE
GOTTA COME THROUGH
DAMN THE PHONE! Yes!

(W1 appears as if on the other end of the line.)

W1.
WELL, HELLO!
W2.
OH, IT'S YOU!

W1. Don't sound so thrilled!
W2. I'm sorry, just crazy busy...

W1.
SO MEET ME FOR LUNCH
W2.
I'M UNDER THE GUN
W1.
YOU STILL HAVE TO EAT, COME ON,
MEET ME AT ONE

W2. Well...
IF YOU GET THERE FIRST
ORDER FOR ME

(W1 anticipates her friend's response and chimes in ...)

W1/W2.
SALAD, NO DRESSING, AND

(W2 realizes W1 is teasing her. She pauses... W1 continues.)

W1.
HERBAL ICED TEA

W2.
 YOU ARE A SMARTASS
W1.
IT'S TRUE; HOW'S YOUR LOVE LIFE?
W2.
JUST FINE, THANKS! AND YOURS?
HAVE YOU ANSWERED HIM YET?

(W1 takes a beat before answering...)

W1.
COME AND
MEET ME FOR LUNCH

W2. What's going on?

W1. One o'clock...
BE THERE OR DIE
SO MUCH TO TELL YOU
W2.
I'LL BE THERE
W1.
'BYE-BYE!

(The phone call ends. Focus shifts to W2.)

W2.
DID SHE SAY "YES?"
WILL THEY BE WED?
IS THIS THE MOMENT
I'VE PICTURED WITH DREAD?
OR MERELY SOME PLOT
SHE NEEDS TO DISCUSS, A
SECRET I'VE GOT TO KEEP
"JUST BETWEEN US"

AND
YES, YES, YES
IT'S SO ODD THAT
DESPITE HOW I'VE GROWN,
COME INTO MY OWN,
AROUND THEM,
I REGRESS

YES, YES, YES

W2. *(Continued)*
IT'S ABSURD, AND
MORE PRESSING THAN LUNCH
ARE THESE NUMBERS TO CRUNCH
AND MY RISING SUCCESS...
YES!

(W1 is now waiting impatiently at a restaurant.)

W1.
TICK-TOCK
TICK-TOCK
    W2.
DAMN IT, I'M LATE, WELL,
SHE KNEW I WOULD BE

(W2 steps into W1's space, joining her at the restaurant.)

W1.
(As if she has already ordered...)
SALAD, NO DRESSING, AND HERBAL ICED TEA!

W2. Sorry! So... what's going on?

W1.
WELL,
THE JOB'S SUBLIME
IT'S A FABULOUS FIT
I LOVE THE PEOPLE AND THE CHALLENGE,
SO EXCITING

W2. And... the big question?

W1.
WELL,
THE TRUTH IS I'M
NOT PREPARED TO COMMIT
AND HE'S UPSET AND I'M CONFUSED AND
WE KEEP FIGHTING

W2. I'm sorry...

W1.
SO AM I!
IT'S A PUZZLE

W1. *(Continued)*
THAT I DON'T UNDERSTAND
I WANT SOMEWHERE TO HIDE
I NEED TIME FOR REFLECTING

I MEAN, WHY
SO MUCH PRESSURE?
EVERY DAY A DEMAND
WHY THE RUSH TO DECIDE?
YOU WOULD THINK HE'S EXPECTING!

W2. He's just in love...

W1.
WELL, YES, I KNOW THAT
I LOVE HIM TOO
BUT...
I NEED A BREAK; SO DOES HE

W2.
IT'S JUST THE JITTERS
W1.
IT'S JUST MY LIFE, LOOK,
COULD YOU DO A FAVOR FOR ME?

W2. What kind of favor?

W1.
SEE, HE DOESN'T KNOW
THAT I'M GOING AWAY
A LITTLE BUSINESS TRIP
ON FRIDAY, OVERNIGHT, THOUGH

W2. So what's the favor?

W1.
WELL,
WITH THE STATUS QUO
IT'S MUCH SIMPLER TO SAY
THAT I'LL BE TRAVELING WITH YOU
IS THAT ALL RIGHT?

W2.
OH...
YOU WANT ME TO LIE?
BUT, I DON'T SEE WHY... Oh ...<u>Is</u> it a business trip?

W1.
YES — YES AND NO
THERE'S THIS CLIENT...
   W2.
I SEE
   W1.
NO, NO YOU DON'T
   W2.
WELL, EXPLAIN IT TO ME

   W1.
NO, NO I WON'T
YOU'RE SUSPICIOUS AS HE
THANKS FOR ASSUMING THE WORST ABOUT ME

YES, YES, YES
IT COULD HAPPEN, WE
AREN'T CEMENTED,
HAVEN'T CONSENTED TO BUY THAT WHITE DRESS

YES,
THERE'S A GUY, I
DON'T KNOW IF I CARE, BUT
THE CHEMISTRY'S THERE, I'M
INTRIGUED, I CONFESS
YES!

   W2.
I CAN'T GO ALONG
YOU KNOW THIS IS WRONG
I'M SORRY
   W1.
ME TOO
   W2.
LOOK, I LOVE BOTH OF YOU...

(*To herself*) YES, YES, YES
THIS IS AWFUL, A
FRIEND WHO'S IN NEED, I
COULD HAVE AGREED TO SUPPORT HER
I GUESS

YES,
BUT BE HONEST
IT'S HIM ON YOUR MIND

W2. *(Continued)*
WITH THOUGHTS YOU'RE INCLINED,
AS A RULE, TO SUPPRESS
YES...

W1.
(To herself) YES, YES, YES,
THIS IS AWFUL, I
THOUGHT SHE'D COMPLY
JUST ONE LITTLE LIE
TO AVOID A BIG MESS
YES...

BUT THE FACT IS
I NEED SOME MORE TIME
IT ISN'T A CRIME
TO APPRAISE AND ASSESS
YES

(MAN enters unexpectedly. His presence pulls the women back into the scene.)

MAN.
THERE YOU ARE! BOTH OF YOU!
HEY, THIS IS GREAT!

W1.
(sotto voce) OH, NO!
   W2. *(sotto voce)* Shit!
(to MAN) HELLO!

W1.
WHAT ARE YOU DOING HERE?
   MAN.
NEWS TO RELATE
   W1.
GOOD OR BAD?
   MAN.
THE BEST!
   W2.
I'M GLAD

MAN.
IT'S WONDERFUL NEWS!

W1.
THAT WE COULD USE… What?

W2. What?

MAN.
WAIT'LL YOU HEAR!
IT'S SO GREAT!

(They wait impatiently as MAN grins, milking the moment.)

W1.
WELL, WE'RE WAITING…
    MAN.
FRIDAY AT SIX

    W1. What?

MAN.
THAT'S WHEN IT CLICKS,
WHEN WE
MIX WITH OUR DESTINY,
CAN'T YOU SEE IT?

    W1. See what?

MAN.
ME, DEBONAIR
YOU, BABE, YOU'RE WEARING AS
DARING A DRESS AS YOU DARE,
SOMETHING THAT'S TASTEFULLY BARE

    W1. Why?

MAN.
(To W1) DINNER
DINNER DATE WITH THE MAN WHO'LL
CHANGE OUR LIFE

    W1. What?

MAN.
DINNER
YOU AND ME WITH OUR FUTURE
AND HIS WIFE

W1.
WHEN DO YOU MEAN?
    MAN.
PICTURE THE SCENE, WE'LL CON-
VENE, FRIDAY NIGHT, AND HE'LL SIGN

    W1/W2. This Friday?

    MAN.
RIGHT ON THE LUCRATIVE LINE
THAT'S WHEN THEY WANT TO MEET
MY FIANCÉE

    W1/W2. Fiancée?

    MAN.
YOU'LL PARADE AND
I'LL PERSUADE AND

(While the women absorb his news, he sings to himself...)

YES, YES, YES,
WHEN SHE SEES ME IN
TOTAL CONTROL AND
SEES ME CAJOLE HIM WITH
CHARM AND FINESSE

YES, YES, YES
I WILL DAZZLE HER
THEN SHE WILL SEE THAT,
THEN SHE'LL AGREE THAT
IT'S TIME TO PROGRESS
YES!

    W1.
(Addressing MAN) WELL, IT'S REALLY GREAT
YOU HOOKED UP WITH THIS MAN
    MAN.
 THIS FINANCIER
    W1.
I'M VERY PROUD
    MAN.
AS YOU SHOULD BE, BABE

(Sensing an impending fight, W2 tries to keep things positive.)

W2. Congratulations!
MAN. (*Oblivious to W1's distress; still preening*) Thank you.

W1. (*Unrelenting*) But...
WHEN YOU MADE THIS DATE
AND CONCOCTED THIS PLAN
DID IT OCCUR TO YOU AT ALL
TO CHECK WITH ME, "BABE?"

    MAN. What?
    W2. (*Bracing for the inevitable explosion*) Oh, God!

W1.
IF YOU'D CHECKED
ABOUT FRIDAY,
THERE'S A FACT YOU'D HAVE KNOWN.
I'LL BE GONE FAR AWAY
SO FORGET HAVING ME THERE

    MAN. What are you talking about?
    W2. (*Instinctively trying to keep the peace, she explains...*) It's
just a business trip...

(*As soon as the words are out, she realizes she has just done what
she said she wouldn't – she has lied to cover for W1. Meanwhile,
W1 barrels ahead. The fight escalates.*)

W1.
WITH RESPECT
TO THAT EVENING
KEEP THE DATE ON YOUR OWN
'CAUSE YOUR SWEET FIANCÉE
WHICH I'M <u>NOT</u>, WILL NOT BE THERE

    MAN.
YOU HAVE TO COME
    W1.
DO I?
    MAN.
YES
    W1.
SAYS WHO?

    MAN. Me!

W1.
NO MATTER WHAT I'D PREFER?
       MAN.
JUST CHANGE YOUR PLANS
THEY'RE EXPECTING YOU
       W1.
THEY'RE EXPECTING A FEMALE
TAKE HER!

(She indicates W2)

       W2/MAN. What!?

       MAN.
WHAT'S THE PROBLEM HERE?
CAN'T YOU GIVE ME A BREAK
AND CHANGE YOUR PLANS?
       W1.
NO, YOU CHANGE YOURS!
       MAN.
I CAN'T!
       W1.
I KNEW IT

       W2. *(Still reeling from W1's suggestion and rejecting any possibility that she would go on the date with MAN, she asserts herself...)*
Look, I can't go...

(W1 and MAN don't even hear her; the fight continues.)

       MAN.
IT'S MY WHOLE CAREER
IT'S OUR FUTURE AT STAKE
I NEED YOU THERE
       W1.
WELL, IF THAT'S TRUE
THEN YOU JUST BLEW IT...

(W1 storms away.)

       MAN.
I DON'T UNDERSTAND
I HAD IT ALL PLANNED
EVERYTHING'S RUINED!

W2.
YOU'LL FIX IT
 MAN.
UNLESS...
COME WITH ME FRIDAY?
 W1.
OH, NO

 MAN.
PLEASE SAY YES!
PLEASE ACQUIESCE
COME AND PRETEND
YOU'RE MY GIRL
BE MY FRIEND

 W2.
IF THEY BELIEVE
I'LL BE YOUR BRIDE
LATER, WHAT THEN?

 MAN.
THEN I'LL TELL THEM YOU DIED
BUT I WON'T LET THIS FIGHT
BLOW MY CHANCES THAT NIGHT

(To himself) WON'T GIVE IN
THIS TIME, I'M GONNA WIN,
YES, YES

 W2.
(To herself) IF I FOLLOW THIS THROUGH
I'LL HELP THEM BOTH
ISN'T THAT TRUE?

 W2/MAN.
YES, YES

 W1. *(To herself, in her own space)*
I'M TIRED OF FEELING OBLIGED TO BE THERE
I HAVE MY OWN LIFE, HIS DEMANDS ARE UNFAIR!

 W2.
(To MAN, deciding to go) YES!
 MAN.
(To W2) YES?

(W2 answers MAN. Simultaneously W1 makes up her mind.)

W2/W1.
YES,
    ALL. *(To themselves)*
IT'S DECIDED
THE EVENING AHEAD
COULD TURN OUT TO BE DREADFUL
BUT NEVERTHELESS

YES, YES, YES
I MUST DO WHAT I
FEEL I MUST DO TO BE
TRUE TO THE PRINCIPLES
THAT I PROFESS
YES!

    W2.
TRUE TO MY FRIENDS
    W1.
TRUE TO MYSELF
    MAN.
TRUE TO MY DREAMS
    ALL.
YES!

(During the musical transition, W1 looks at MAN and W2. They each turn away, leaving her to contemplate her decision.)

NOCTURNE *(Reprise)*
    W1.
IT ISN'T LIKE THIS TRIP WILL END US FOREVER
I DOUBT THAT IT COULD
IT'S ONLY THAT I NEED TO KNOW
IT'S REALLY WHY I HAVE TO GO
TO KNOW...

(The focus shifts to MAN and W2, just prior to the business dinner. MAN is nervously coaching W2 for the evening ahead.)

THE SCHMOOZE

MAN.
THEY'RE FROM MONTPELIER
HE OWNS HALF THE STATE

W2. Right!

MAN.
HIS NAME IS NATHAN,
DO NOT CALL HIM NATE

W2. Check!

MAN.
HER NAME IS KATYA,
PLEASE, DON'T CALL HER KATE

W2. Yup!

MAN.
THEY CAN MAKE WAITING
A VERY SHORT WAIT
SO, LAUGH AT HIS JOKES
FLATTER HIS WIFE
REMEMBER, IT'S ONLY
THE REST OF MY LIFE

BUT DON'T BE TOO PUSHY
DON'T COME ON TOO STRONG
REMEMBER I TOLD THEM WE PLAN TO BE MARRIED
SO IF IT COMES UP
PLAY ALONG

(They sit down to dinner and address the other, unseen couple.)

W2.
FABULOUS DRESS
SHALL I GUESS?
OF COURSE, IT'S CHANEL
IT'S "LABELS FOR LESS"
YOU'RE KIDDING ME, YES?
WELL, NO ONE COULD TELL
ON YOU, IT'S CHANEL!

(MAN attempts to pick up where W2 left off...)

MAN.
DYNAMITE TIE
GRABS THE EYE

(In her nervousness, W2 can't stop babbling and interrupts him ...)

W2.
AND DOESN'T LET GO
IT BRISTLES WITH CLOUT
IT LEAVES NOT A DOUBT
THAT YOU'RE YOUR OWN GUY –

(They realize W2 has made a faux pas, as she repeats "Nathan's" response...)

W2.
THE RESTAURANT'S TIE? *(She perseveres...)*

I'LL HAVE WHAT YOU'RE DRINKING
I LOVE SCOTCH AND SPRITE
I COULD DRINK IT ALL NIGHT
BON APPETITE! –

(She corrects herself, using the French pronunciation this time.)

W2. Teet –
MAN. *(As if he's asking "How could you have mispronounced that?")* Tite?

(She surreptitiously takes a big swig of her drink, trying to hide her distaste for the combination of Scotch and Sprite. He focuses on the other couple, continuing the small talk.)

MAN.
YOU'RE FROM VERMONT
WHO COULD WANT
A LOVELIER STATE

(W2 chimes in once again, slightly feeling the effects of the Scotch.)

W2.
THIS TOWN'S ON THE SKIDS
THEY SHOOT LITTLE KIDS,
IT'S TRUE

MAN.
IT GIVES A NEW MEANING TO URBAN DECAY
   W2.
SMALL WONDER THAT PEOPLE ARE MOVING AWAY
FLEEING IN FEAR
   MAN.
YOU BOUGHT A HOUSE HERE?
   BOTH.
TODAY!

(Horrified, they look at each other, then face the other couple, as if in response to a question.)

   W2.
WEDDING PLANS?
WHAT WEDDING PLANS?
WHOSE WEDDING?

(MAN puts his arm around her shoulders and gives her a "reminder" hug. She gets the message.)

   W2.
OH, YOU MEAN MINE!
RIGHT AWAY
   MAN.
MOST ANY DAY NOW
   W2.
MONDAY!
COME RAIN OR SHINE
WAITER, PLEASE
ANOTHER OF THESE
BUT NOT SO MUCH SPRITE
NATE — NAT — NATHANIEL

   MAN. Nathan!

   W2.
(To MAN, losing her cool.) RIGHT!

(The waiter delivers her drink. She takes a big swig. He keeps trying...)

   MAN.
FEELS LIKE A STORM
VERY WARM
FOR THIS TIME OF YEAR

W2.
IT'S MORE LIKE JULY
   BOTH.
A NEAR RECORD HIGH
I HEAR
   MAN.
PERHAPS WE SHOULD ORDER

   W2.
(Going for broke) AND SPEAKING OF GRANTS
SHOULD WE FOUR BE RAISING A TOAST IN ADVANCE?
DOES SOMEONE WE KNOW
STAND A GHOST OF A CHANCE?
I JUST BLEW IT, RIGHT?

   MAN.
YOU'RE MUCH TOO POLITE
   BOTH.
NO MORE SCOTCH AND SPRITE
   W2.
FOR ME

*(Throughout the next section, he tries to take the conversational
   lead, but she won't let him get a word in...)*

   BOTH.
SO --
   W2.
GRANTED, I SHOULDN'T HAVE
BROUGHT UP THE GRANT
   BOTH.
DON'T
   W2.
KNOW WHO'S MORE POTTED,
MYSELF OR THAT PLANT

   BOTH.
PLEASE,
   W2.
EVEN IF YOU COULD FORGIVE ME I CAN'T
BUT I GUARANTEE
NO MORE THIRD DEGREE
QUEL PUSHY OF ME TO PRESS

(She stops short as if listening intently. MAN perks up.)

MAN.
YOU'RE DRINKING TO WHO?
   W2.
(To MAN) THEY'RE DRINKING TO YOU
      BOTH.
I KNEW YOU COULD DO IT

(They watch the other couple leave, then they too exit the restaurant, each feeling triumphant.)

   BOTH.
YES!

(In their excitement, they kiss. The music and lights change. She pulls out of the kiss, but he remains frozen as if time is suspended. We hear W2's internal thoughts as she sings…)

TAKE THE WORLD AWAY

   W2.
OH, MY GOD…

OH, PLEASE
TAKE THE WORLD AWAY
OH, PLEASE
MAKE HIM LONG TO STAY IN THIS DREAM
MAKE IT LAST, I PRAY
TAKE THE WORLD AWAY

OH, PLEASE
FOR A SINGLE NIGHT
OH, PLEASE
CAN'T I HAVE THE RIGHT TO DO WRONG?
HOW I WISH I MIGHT
TAKE THE WORLD AWAY

FOR ONCE
CAN'T I, ONCE, BE RASH AND WILD?
FOR ONCE
BE A RECKLESS FOOL?
FOR ONCE,
CAN'T HE READ MY MIND?
CAN'T I TAKE THE LEAD?
LET MY PASSIONS RULE?

W2. *(Continued)*
OH, PLEASE
IF IT'S MEANT TO BE
OH, PLEASE
LET HIM LOOK AND SEE ALL MY DREAMS
ARE OF HIM WITH ME
TAKE THE WORLD AWAY

OH, PLEASE
MAKE TODAY THE DAY
TAKE THE WORLD AWAY

(She leans in and kisses him, resuming the embrace as if it had never stopped. He kisses back, but then abruptly breaks it off.)

HOMEWORK (Reprise II)

(After an awkward, pregnant pause, he attempts to ignore what just happened.)

MAN.
WELL, THANKS, WHAT A FRIEND!
W2.
(Crushed, but covering) OH, SURE...
MAN.
YOU WERE GREAT!
W2.
NO PROBLEM, OLD FRIEND
(Desperate to get away) GOOD NIGHT

MAN.
WHAT?
W2.
IT'S LATE
MAN.
IT IS?
W2. Uh-huh
'BYE
MAN.
'BYE

(She quickly leaves. He begins talking to himself, trying to calm himself down.)

OKAY

MAN.
OKAY,
OKAY,
OKAY!

TAKE A BREATH AND GET YOUR BEARINGS
OKAY,
SCREW YOUR HEAD ON STRAIGHT AND QUICK

MAN, YOU KNOW THAT SUCH A PAIRING'S
TOO OUTRAGEOUS TO CONSIDER
SHE'S LIKE FAMILY WHICH MEANS YOU'RE SICK!

OKAY
IT'S BECAUSE OF ALL THE WORRY
AND WAY
TOO MUCH SCOTCH AND STRESS AND SPRITE

BUT SHE LEFT IN SUCH A HURRY
COULD SHE TELL WHAT I WAS FEELING?
DID IT SHOCK HER SO THAT SHE TOOK FLIGHT?

THIS IS MORONIC!
WE'VE BEEN BUDDIES SINCE THE EARTH WAS FLAT
PURELY PLATONIC
IF I'D KNOWN THAT SHE COULD KISS LIKE THAT!
GOTTA GET A GRIP
NIP IT IN THE —
THIS IS TOO ABSURD
PLUS, NOTHING HAPPENED
NOTHING MEANINGFUL OCCURRED

OKAY
MAKE AN EFFORT TO RECOVER
OKAY
GET THE HORMONE RUSH TO HALT!

COULD THIS BE BECAUSE MY LOVER
LEFT ME ALL ALONE THIS EVENING?
YES, IT COULD
IN FACT, IT'S ALL HER FAULT!

IF SHE HAD STAYED HERE

MAN. *(Continued)*
THESE EMOTIONS WOULD HAVE
NEVER SEEN THE LIGHT
AND IF I STRAYED HERE
WHO COULD BLAME ME, IT MIGHT
EVEN SERVE HER RIGHT
EVEN THOUGH IT'S WRONG
WHAT THE HELL IS —
THIS IS SO DERANGED
SINCE NOTHING HAPPENED
NOT A SINGLE THING HAS CHANGED

OKAY,
GET A GRIP OR MEDICATION
OKAY?
AND IF ALL ELSE FAILS, THEN PRAY

THAT THIS LINGERING SENSATION
IS A PASSING ABERRATION
GOD, I WISH SHE HADN'T GONE AWAY

I DON'T WANT TO BE ALONE NOW
BUT THE ONE I WANT TO PHONE NOW
WOULD BE HER, AND THAT IS NOT
OKAY!

IF YOU ONLY KNEW

(Lights up on W1, in her own space.)

W1.
WELL, IF
ANYONE TOLD ME YESTERDAY
HOW I'D FEEL IN THE MORNING LIGHT
I PROBABLY WOULD HAVE LAUGHED OUT LOUD
AT THE THOUGHT I'D REGRET LAST NIGHT

BUT, I HAVE TO CONFRONT THE SIMPLE TRUTH
THOUGH IT COMES WITH A NASTY STING
WHAT I HOPED MIGHT BECOME A NEW ROMANCE
WAS FOR HIM JUST A ONE NIGHT THING

NOW, THE LOVE THAT I BRUSHED AWAY
OH, HOW PRECIOUS IT SEEMS TODAY...

(Referring to MAN) IF YOU ONLY KNEW

W2. *(Continued)*
HOW MUCH I HAVE LEARNED
ABOUT MYSELF AND
ME AND YOU
WOULD YOU UNDERSTAND?

ALL MY PETTY ANGER
ALL MY PRIDE AND GREED, ALL GONE
ALL I FEEL IS SORRY
IF YOU ONLY KNEW
COULD WE GO ON?

IF YOU ONLY KNEW
LEFT YOU, OH, SO BRIEFLY
BUT THE CHANGES I'VE BEEN THROUGH
SINCE THEN
MAYBE YOU'D FORGIVE ME...

(Focus on W2, in her own space, also referring to MAN.)

W2.
IF YOU ONLY KNEW
ALL THE SECRETS HELD
I WONDER
WHAT YOU'D WANT TO DO
WHO YOU'D WANT TO LOVE

I WAS SUCH A COWARD
WHEN I RAN AWAY LAST NIGHT
WHY THIS DAMN COMPULSION
TO BE SURE I DO   **W1.**
WHAT'S FAIR AND RIGHT?   IF YOU ONLY KNEW
IF YOU ONLY KNEW
ALL THE LOVE I'M SAVING
LOVE SO STRONG, SO DEEP,
SO OVERDUE
MAYBE THEN YOU'D SEE ME   MAYBE YOU'D FORGIVE ME
IF YOU ONLY KNEW
SEE ME AND PERHAPS LOVE ME TOO

W2/W1.
IF YOU ONLY KNEW

(Focus on MAN in his own space, referring to W1.)

MAN.
IF YOU ONLY KNEW
I FEEL SO DISLOYAL
WHICH IS CRAZY,
BUT IT'S TRUE   **W1/W2.**
HELP ME UNDERSTAND   IF YOU ONLY KNEW

WHY THIS STRAIN BETWEEN US?
HOW DID ALL OUR TROUBLES START?
DON'T YOU KNOW I LOVE YOU
AND I HATE THE WAY WE'VE GROWN APART

ALL.
IF YOU ONLY KNEW
WHAT A FOOL I FEEL
I WISH I KNEW EXACTLY WHAT
TO DO

MAN.
WOULD YOU UNDERSTAND ME?   **W1.**
                                WOULD YOU UNDERSTAND
                                ME?

W2.
COULD YOU SEE WHAT'S TRUE?
ALL.
WOULD YOU SEE HOW MUCH I LOVE YOU?
W1.
IF YOU
W2.
IF YOU
MAN.
IF YOU
ALL.
IF YOU ONLY KNEW

LITTLE BY LITTLE IV

W1.
HIDING OUR FEELINGS,
MAN/W1.
AFRAID THEY MIGHT SHOW
FIGHTING TO HOLD ON,

ALL.
AFRAID TO LET GO
DREADING THE DAY WHEN WE JUST OVERFLOW
ON AN EMOTIONAL ROLL
W2.
FRIGHTENED WE'RE OUT OF CONTROL

YES (Reprise)

(W1 approaches MAN.)

W1.
HI
MAN.
HI
W1.
SO GLAD TO SEE YOU
MAN.
YOU MEAN THAT?
W1.
OH, YES

(Awkward pause)

BOTH.
HOW WAS YOUR EVENING?

W1. You first...

MAN.
BIG SUCCESS

W1. See — you didn't need me!
MAN. Actually, she went as you...

W1. Oh... well...
IT'S WONDERFUL NEWS...

(She hugs him. He returns the embrace, then breaks it.)

MAN. How did your trip go?

W1.
NOT AS I PLANNED

MAN. Why?

W1.
LOOK, TO BE CANDID, I'VE
LANDED MYSELF IN A MESS,
CONFESSION TIME
I'VE BEEN A FOOL
I HOPE THAT YOU'LL KEEP YOUR
COOL WHEN I TELL YOU WHAT HAPPENED

MAN.
TELL ME
W1.
FEELINGS
I'VE BEEN HAVING THESE FEELINGS
FOR THIS GUY
MAN.
FEELINGS?
W1.
YES, THESE SEXUAL FEELINGS
MAN.
SO HAVE I!

W1. What?

MAN.
NOT FOR A GUY!

W1. For who?

MAN.   I DON'T KNOW WHY
BUT, WHEN I, WELL,
WHEN SHE AND I KISSED

W1. What?

MAN.
FEELINGS AROSE THAT PERSIST

W1. You kissed her?

MAN.
I'VE BEEN A TOTAL WRECK
GUESS YOU HAVE TOO
I'M SO GLAD
WE BOTH FEEL BAD...

(He comes toward her as if to take her in his arms. She steps back away from him, still processing her feelings of betrayal and shock.)

IF YOU LOVED ME

W1.
IF YOU LOVED ME, HONESTLY LOVED ME
HOW COULD THIS OCCUR?

MAN. What?

W1.
IF YOU LOVED ME, TOTALLY LOVED ME
HOW COULD YOU KISS HER?

MAN. But nothing happened!

W1.
NEVER ONCE DID I SURMISE
NEVER! WHAT A SWEET SURPRISE
YOU ARE NOT THE MAN I THOUGHT YOU WERE!
IF YOU LOVED ME

MAN.
YOU KNOW THAT I LOVE YOU
LET ME PLEASE EXPLAIN
W1.
IF YOU LOVED ME
MAN.
GOD DAMN IT, I DO
W1.
NO NEED TO BE PROFANE
MAN. Shit!

W1.
HOPE YOU'RE GLAD FOR WHAT YOU'VE DONE
HOPE YOU HAD A LOT OF FUN
MAN.
STOP IT!
W1.
GO TO HELL!
MAN.
THIS IS INSANE!
YOU SAID YOU HAD FEELINGS TOO
SO CAN'T YOU COMPREHEND?

W1.
NO!
I DID NOT HAVE FEELINGS
FOR YOUR OLDEST, DEAREST FRIEND

MAN.
BUT,
NOTHING HAPPENED
   W1.
DON'T BELIEVE YOU
   MAN.
BUT IT'S TRUE
   W1.
KISSING ISN'T NOTHING
SO, DID SHE HAVE FEELINGS TOO?

MAN.
NO!
IF YOU LOVED ME...
YOU'D TRY TO UNDERSTAND ... Please!

W1.
IF YOU LOVED ME...
TELL ME, WAS THIS PLANNED?

MAN.
WHAT A LOUSY THING TO SAY
   W1.
OH, WAS WHAT YOU DID OKAY?
   MAN.
NO,
BUT THIS IS GETTING OUT OF HAND

MAN.
IF YOU LOVED ME...
   W1.
IF YOU LOVED ME...

(They part)

W1.
(To herself) GREAT, THIS IS GREAT,
WHAT A HATEFUL THING
BETRAYED BY MISS PROPER-AND-PRIM

W1. *(Continued)*
(She confronts W2) FRIEND, WHAT A FRIEND!
WELL, DEPEND ON THIS —
OUR FRIENDSHIP IS DEAD

W2.
WHAT IS THIS?
    W1.
IT'S DEAD AND BURIED!
FINISHED!

W2.
WHAT THE HELL IS GOING ON?
    W1.
DON'T PRETEND YOU'RE INNOCENT,
HE TOLD ME THAT YOU KISSED

    W2. He what?

W1.
DON'T BE COY, YOU PLANNED IT,
YOU ARRANGED THIS LITTLE TRYST

    W2. No! It wasn't like that...

W1.
AFTER I EXPLAINED TO YOU
ALL THAT I WAS GOING THROUGH
GONE FOR JUST ONE NIGHT, LOOK WHAT I MISSED!

(MAN enters. They don't see him as he listens to their confrontation.)

    W2.
HOW COULD YOU ACCUSE ME?
WE'VE BEEN FRIENDS OUR WHOLE LIVES LONG
    W1.
HOW COULD YOU ABUSE MY TRUST?
SOME FRIEND!
    W2.
OH, NO, YOU'RE WRONG
IT'S YOU WHO HAS ABUSED A TRUST
HOW WAS YOUR AFFAIR?
DID YOU FIND YOUR ANSWER?
DID YOU?
HOW DID HE COMPARE?

W2. *(Continued)*
DID YOU DO IT?
W1.
NONE OF YOUR BUSINESS
W2.
OH, MY GOD, YOU DID!
W1.
IF I DID, IT'S
NONE OF YOUR BUSINESS
W2.
YOU MADE IT MY BUSINESS

(MAN steps into the scene, confronting them ...)

MAN.
IS IT MY BUSINESS?
IS IT THE TRUTH?

W1. Yes

MAN. *(to W2)*
AND YOU KNEW IT...
W2. Yes...

MAN. *(to W1, throwing her words back at her)*
IF YOU LOVED ME...
W1. *(to W2, transferring the blame)*
IF YOU LOVED ME...
MAN. *(also to W2)*
IF YOU LOVED ME...

I'M NOT (Reprise)

(Stunned that they've both turned on her.)

W2.
EXCUSE ME IF I ASK YOU BOTH, HOW DARE YOU?
JUST WHAT THE HELL DO YOU THINK FRIENDS ARE FOR?
W2.
CONDEMNING ME WHEN ALL I'VE DONE IS SPARE YOU
WELL, GUESS WHAT — NO MORE!

(MAN tries to say something. She stops him cold.)

W2.
NOT A WORD
YOU LISTEN GOOD!
I'M SICK OF THIS ETERNAL SQUEEZE
WITH BOTH OF YOU TO TRY TO PLEASE
I'VE HAD IT AND THE FACTS ARE THESE.

(To W1.) THAT YOU, FRIEND,
YOU ARE SELFISHNESS DEFINED
(To MAN.) AND YOU, PAL,
YOU'RE AS DENSE AS YOU ARE BLIND

(To both.) I'M NOT,
WELL, I WAS BUT NOW I'M THROUGH
I WON'T ACCEPT THE BLAME
FOR YOUR GUILT OR GRIEF OR SHAME
SO THAT'S IT NOW
I QUIT NOW
I USED TO CARE A LOT
WHEN WE WERE FRIENDS, BUT NOW
WE'RE NOT!

(She leaves.)

TELL ME

(Alone with W1, he struggles to express all his conflicting emotions.)

MAN.
TELL ME HOW TO TELL YOU WHAT I'M FEELING
TELL ME WHAT YOU THINK I OUGHT TO SAY
YOU'RE THE ONE WHO ALWAYS HAS THE ANSWERS
TELL ME HOW YOU THINK THIS SCENE SHOULD PLAY

TELL ME WHY I TRUSTED THAT YOU LOVED ME
TELL ME HOW I OVERLOOKED EACH CLUE
WAS I REALLY THAT NAIVE?
OR DID I NEED TO MAKE BELIEVE?
OR DID I THINK MY LOVE COULD MAKE IT TRUE?

THE WORDS YOU ALWAYS WHISPER,
WORDS I ALWAYS LOVE TO HEAR
THOSE TENDER, LOVING PHRASES
SO IMPASSIONED, SO SINCERE...

MAN. *(Continued)*
TELL ME ONCE AGAIN THAT YOU ADORE ME
TELL ME ALL THE SPECIAL REASONS WHY
TELL ME SWEETLY FACE TO FACE
HOW NO ONE ELSE CAN TAKE MY PLACE
TELL ME ONCE AGAIN THAT LOVELY LIE

TELL ME HOW IT FEELS TO HEAR ME TELL YOU
GOOD-BYE

(He leaves.)

I OUGHT TO CRY

(Alone, she faces up to what she has done.)

W1.
WELL, I SUPPOSE I OUGHT TO CRY
FOR GOODNESS KNOWS
THAT'S WHAT A NORMAL GIRL WOULD DO
SHED A TEAR OR TWO
FOR LOVE
FOR LOVE GONE BY, BUT
CAN'T EVEN BRING MYSELF TO SIGH

CAN'T SHED A SINGLE TEAR AND SUDDENLY I KNOW
SUDDENLY, ALTHOUGH
IT'S NO SURPRISE

I TOOK HIS LOVE FOR GRANTED, MINE FOREVER
HE COULDN'T LEAVE; HE WOULDN'T DARE
NO MATTER WHAT I DID OR HOW I HURT HIM
I HAD TO PROVE HE'D ALWAYS CARE

AND NOW I KNOW I OUGHT TO CRY
MY LITTLE GAMES HAVE BEEN AS POINTLESS AS CAN BE
WHY SO LONG TO SEE
SOMETHING'S WRONG WITH ME

WELL, I CAN CHANGE
OR IS THAT JUST ANOTHER LIE?
I OUGHT TO KNOW
I OUGHT TO TRY
I OUGHT TO CRY

LITTLE BY LITTLE V

(With a new energy, they attempt to rebuild their lives.)

W2.
LITTLE BY LITTLE
   W2/MAN.
LITTLE BY LITTLE
   MAN/W1.
LITTLE BY LITTLE
   ALL.
LITTLE BY LITTLE

LITTLE BY LITTLE YOU'RE FACED WITH THE FACT
THIS IS YOUR LIFE AND THERE'S NO SECOND ACT
IT'S UP TO YOU TO GET THROUGH IT INTACT
NO ONE CAN LIVE IT BUT YOU
LITTLE BY LITTLE, YOU DO

SO IT GOES

(Time is passing; life goes on. The three former friends, each in their own worlds, remark on how their lives have changed.)

   ALL.
MY LIFE IS BRIMMING, BUZZING
NEW PASTIMES BY THE SCORE
   W1.
I'M CATCHING EVERY BALLGAME;
EACH MOVIE FILLED WITH GORE!
   W2.
I'VE STARTED PUMPING IRON
   MAN.
I'VE CONQUERED PASTRY DOUGHS
   ALL.
BECOMING MUCH MORE ROUNDED AND IT SHOWS
SO IT GOES

NEW PALS, NEW DATES, NEW PROJECTS
   W1.
GOLF!
   W2.
HIP-HOP!
   MAN.
MACRAMÉ!

W2/W1.
EACH DAY'S A NEW ADVENTURE
    MAN.
EACH NIGHT'S A PASSION PLAY
    ALL.
WITH EVERY WEEK THAT PASSES
MY INDEPENDENCE GROWS
I MEAN, I'M LIKE A HUMAN BLOOMING ROSE
SO IT GOES

MEETING LOTS OF PEOPLE AND I'M BRANCHING OUT LIKE MAD
    W1.
GOING, SEEING, DOING,
    W2.
HAVING FUN I'VE NEVER HAD
    MAN.
I'M THE LEADING MONARCH OF THE SOCIAL BUTTERFLIES
    ALL.
BOY, IF THEY COULD SEE ME,
THEY WOULD NOT BELIEVE THEIR EYES!

    ALL.
MY DATE LAST NIGHT, INTRIGUING
CHOCK FULL OF CHARM AND QUIPS
    W2.
HE WORE THE COOLEST EARRINGS
PIERCED THROUGH HIS TONGUE AND LIPS
    MAN.
SHE WAS A BRILLIANT WOMAN
BUT THEN SHE PICKED HER NOSE
    W1.
IF NOT FOR HIS OBSESSION WITH MY TOES — !
    ALL.
SO IT GOES

THE PHONE THAT RINGS WITH FIX-UPS
THERE'S NO ESCAPE, I FEAR
    W1.
MY BOSS'S SISTER'S DENTIST
WITH HAIR COMBED EAR-TO-EAR
    W2.
MY NEIGHBOR'S SON, THE SHRINK WHO
LIKES WEARING PANTYHOSE
    MAN.
MY BARBER'S TWO-TON NIECE IN SKIN-TIGHT CLOTHES

ALL.
SO IT GOES

I WILL BET MY FORMER FRIENDS ARE HAVING GRAND AFFAIRS
   W1.
SHE IS DATING GENIUSES
   W2.
SHE'S JUGGLING BILLIONAIRES
   MAN.
BET THEY'RE BOTH SO HAPPY;
BET THEY'RE GLAD THEY'RE RID OF ME
   ALL.
BET THEY BOTH HAVE LEARNED HOW LOVE AND FRIENDSHIP
   OUGHT TO BE

(The mood shifts. Their continuing sense of sadness and loss surfaces.)

   W1/MAN.
CAN'T FIND A FRIEND TO TALK TO
NOT LIKE I COULD WITH HER

   W2.
WHAT IF THEY'RE BACK TOGETHER
AS CLOSE AS THEY ONCE WERE?
   ALL.
I'VE GOT THIS NIGHTMARE FEELING
I'VE LOST A PRICELESS GIFT
I'M WIDE AWAKE AT LAST, GOD KNOWS
BUT

THEY HAVEN'T MISSED ME, I SUPPOSE
AND
SO IT GOES,
SO IT GOES,
SO IT GOES

POPCORN II

*(All three file into seats at the movies. He holds a big box of pop-
corn. On the accents of the music, they discover one another –
first MAN and W2, then MAN and W1, then the two women.
They sink into their seats, incredulous, exploring their separate
thoughts and feelings.)*

ALL.
I DO NOT BELIEVE THAT THIS IS HAPPENING!
   W1/W2.
BOTH AT ONCE! AND WHEN I LOOK LIKE SHIT!
   MAN.
SEVEN ZILLION SEATS TO CHOOSE FROM AND THEY SIT
RIGHT NEXT TO ME!
   ALL.
YES, I GUESS IT COULD BE PURE COINCIDENCE
INDEPENDENTLY WE CHANCED TO PICK
TUESDAY AFTERNOON TO CATCH THE SAME DAMN FLICK

   W2/W1.
DID SHE KNOW
HE WAS GONNA BE HERE?
THAT WOULD MAKE MY DAY
   MAN.
DID THEY FOLLOW ME HERE?
   ALL.
SHOULD I GO OR STAY?

   MAN.
ALL THE TIMES THAT I RELIVED EACH MOMENT AND
THOUGHT OF BRILLIANT THINGS TO SAY
SO, COME ON, SO WHERE'S THAT SNAPPY REPARTÉE?

I COULD OFFER THEM SOME POPCORN
THEY COULD TAKE IT OR REFUSE
THEY ALREADY HATE MY GUTS,
SO WHAT'S TO LOSE?

*(He contemplates passing the popcorn to W1, then abruptly decides
   on W2. In her surprise and nervousness, she begins compulsively
   eating the popcorn as W1 observes.)*

   W1.
WHY'S HE PASSING IT TO HER, INSTEAD OF ME?
DON'T BE DUMB, YOU KNOW EXACTLY WHY
FUNNY HOW THEY ALWAYS DID SEE EYE TO EYE
I HATED THAT

   W2.
CAREFUL, DON'T GO READING TOO MUCH INTO THIS
FRIENDLY OVERTURE AND NOTHING MORE
DON'T YOU DARE BECOME A DOORMAT LIKE BEFORE

(She defiantly throws back the popcorn that was in her hand.)

MAN.
DON'T PANIC
FIGURE OUT YOUR FEELINGS
(He looks at W1) WHAT EMOTIONS STIR?
NOT A SHRED OF LONGING;
(He looks at W2) BUT WHAT ABOUT HER?
COULD THIS MEETING BE A DATE WITH DESTINY?

(MAN passes the popcorn back to W2. She cautiously takes some.)

W2.
COULD THIS BE A TRICK OF FATE?
W1.
WELL, TO HELL WITH IT! LET HER PUT ON THE WEIGHT!

(Not wanting to hurt W1, MAN passes the popcorn to her too. W2 observes and cautions herself.)

W2.
SEE, HE'S PASSING HER THE POPCORN
DON'T ASSUME IT'S OVER YET
W1.
NOT MUCH LEFT, BUT I WILL TAKE WHAT I CAN GET

(W1 gratefully eats some popcorn. MAN begins to pass the box back and forth as all three dig in.)

ALL.
AS LONG AS
WE KEEP PASSING POPCORN
THERE'S AN OPEN LINE
THERE'S COMMUNICATION
AND THAT'S A GOOD SIGN
W2. *(Reaching in and coming up empty.)*
HOW MUCH LONGER CAN WE KEEP ON DOING THIS
WHEN WE KNOW THAT WE'VE RUN OUT?
YEAH, BUT ISN'T THAT WHAT THIS IS ALL ABOUT

(She goes back for "more." They all realize the box is empty but MAN keeps passing it and they all keep pretending to eat.)

W2/W1.
WHEN YOU WANNA NURSE A FRIENDSHIP

W2/W1. *(Continued)*
THAT'S BECOME A LITTLE SICK
FUNNY HOW A LITTLE POPCORN DOES THE TRICK

ALL.
NOTHING LIKE A LITTLE POPCORN
WHEN A FRIENDSHIP'S ON THE ROCKS
EVEN WHEN YOU KNOW THERE'S NOTHING IN THE BOX!

(On the final note of the song, as they grab for the popcorn once more, their hands connect. Now, they sing to each other, no longer at the movies.)

I'M A ROTTEN PERSON

W1.
I'M...
MAN.
I'M...
W2.
I'M...

W1.
I'M A ROTTEN PERSON
I MEAN IT, ROTTEN TO THE CORE
I RUINED EVERYTHING AND
I DO UNDERSTAND
WE'LL NEVER BE LIKE BEFORE

I'VE BEEN A
SELFISH, ROTTEN PERSON
WHICH ISN'T HOW I MEANT TO LIVE
SO, LET ME PLEASE MAKE AMENDS
I WANT TO BE FRIENDS
I HOPE YOU CAN BOTH FORGIVE

MAN.
THAT'S NOT SO EASY
W1.
I KNOW IT'S NOT
W2.
NO, IT'S NOT
W1.
AGREED!
NO, IT'S NOT EASY
BUT IF I GROVEL AND BEG AND PLEAD?

W1. *(Continued)*
REPEATING I'M A
DEEPLY ROTTEN PERSON
NO OTHER WORD FOR ME APPLIES
I'M REALLY SORRY, I AM
AND DAMN. HOW I MISS YOU GUYS

MAN.
(To W1) IT'S TRUE THAT
YOU'RE A ROTTEN PERSON
YOU'RE REALLY GOOD, THE BEST, A PRO
BUT I'M OBLIGED TO ADMIT
WE TWO DIDN'T FIT
WE'D NEVER HAVE WORKED
W1.
I KNOW

MAN.
(To W2) THE FACT IS
I'M A ROTTEN PERSON
I WAS A LOUSY FRIEND TO YOU
TO TRY TO MAKE IT YOUR FAULT
THAT VERBAL ASSAULT
I'M SORRY FOR THAT

W1.
(To W2) ME TOO
(To both) WE COULD START OVER
PERHAPS RECAPTURE OUR GOLDEN YOUTH

ALL.
(Thinking it through) WE COULD START OVER
W1.
IF WE BEGIN WITH A VOW OF TRUTH...
(MAN and W2 stop and stare at W1. Deciding to trust W1's sincerity... MAN agrees.)

MAN.
OKAY

(Weighing the impact of agreeing, W2 decides it's time at last to reveal her secret feelings.)

W2.
OKAY...

W2. *(Continued)*
THEN...
I'M A ROTTEN PERSON
   W1.
NO, YOU'RE A SAINT!
   W2.
NO, THAT'S NOT TRUE
THERE IS A
SECRET I'VE KEPT
FOR YEAR AFTER YEAR
BUT NOW, WELL, THE TRUTH COMES DUE

I'M A ROTTEN PERSON
FOR ONE AWFUL REASON
(To W1) I LOVE HIM
(To MAN) I'VE ALWAYS LOVED YOU

(W2 moves toward MAN as if to kiss him. She stops abruptly when she realizes that he is staring at her in disbelief. She steps away and averts her gaze.)

*(**STARLIGHT** music is heard. All three resume their positions from the first time they sang **STARLIGHT**, as if remembering that decisive moment in their lives.)*

STARLIGHT (Reprise)

   ALL.
STARLIGHT
STARBRIGHT
FIRST STAR I SEE TONIGHT...

(MAN and W1 exchange looks. W1 looks away, smiling at the inevitable. Released and relieved, MAN turns hopefully to W2, just at the same moment she is turning toward him. They come together and kiss.)

   MAN.
OH, MY GOD
   W2.
OH, YES, YES. YE...

(So excited he can't wait for her to finish the word, MAN cuts her off with another kiss. She joyfully returns his ardor. W1 observes and comments.)

A JOURNEY THAT NEVER ENDS

W1.
RIGHT NOW
EVERYTHING BEGINS TO BE CLEAR
AND THOUGH WE CAN'T BE SURE WHERE WE GO FROM HERE
IT SEEMS WE'RE ON
A JOURNEY THAT NEVER ENDS

W2/MAN.
RIGHT NOW
LIFE PRESENTS A STUNNING NEW TWIST
AS LOVE REVEALS A PATH THAT WE ALMOST MISSED
ALL.
WE MUST BE ON
A JOURNEY THAT NEVER ENDS
W1/W2.
THESE ARE THE PEOPLE
MAN.
THE ONLY TWO PEOPLE
ALL.
I'VE ALWAYS WANTED CLOSE AT HAND
NOW, AT LAST, I UNDERSTAND
THESE ARE MY FRIENDS, BUT
TO FLOURISH AS FRIENDS, WE MUST GROW
GROW TO SEE THAT

NO,
LIFE WON'T BE THE WAY WE SUPPOSED
AND LOVE HAS MANY LAYERS TO BE DISCLOSED
AND THOUGH WE'VE CHANGED
AND REARRANGED
I HOPE WE'RE ON
A JOURNEY THAT NEVER ENDS
MAN.
WE'LL LEARN AGAIN
W1/W2.
LITTLE BY LITTLE
MAN.
TO EARN AGAIN
W1/W2.
LITTLE BY LITTLE
ALL.
THE FRIENDS WE ONCE WERE WORTHY OF

LITTLE BY LITTLE

ALL. *(Continued)*
LITTLE BY LITTLE
LITTLE BY LITTLE
WE LOVE

*(Without having to look, the three extend their hands and their hands
      join, a symbol of their friendship and love.)*

CURTAIN

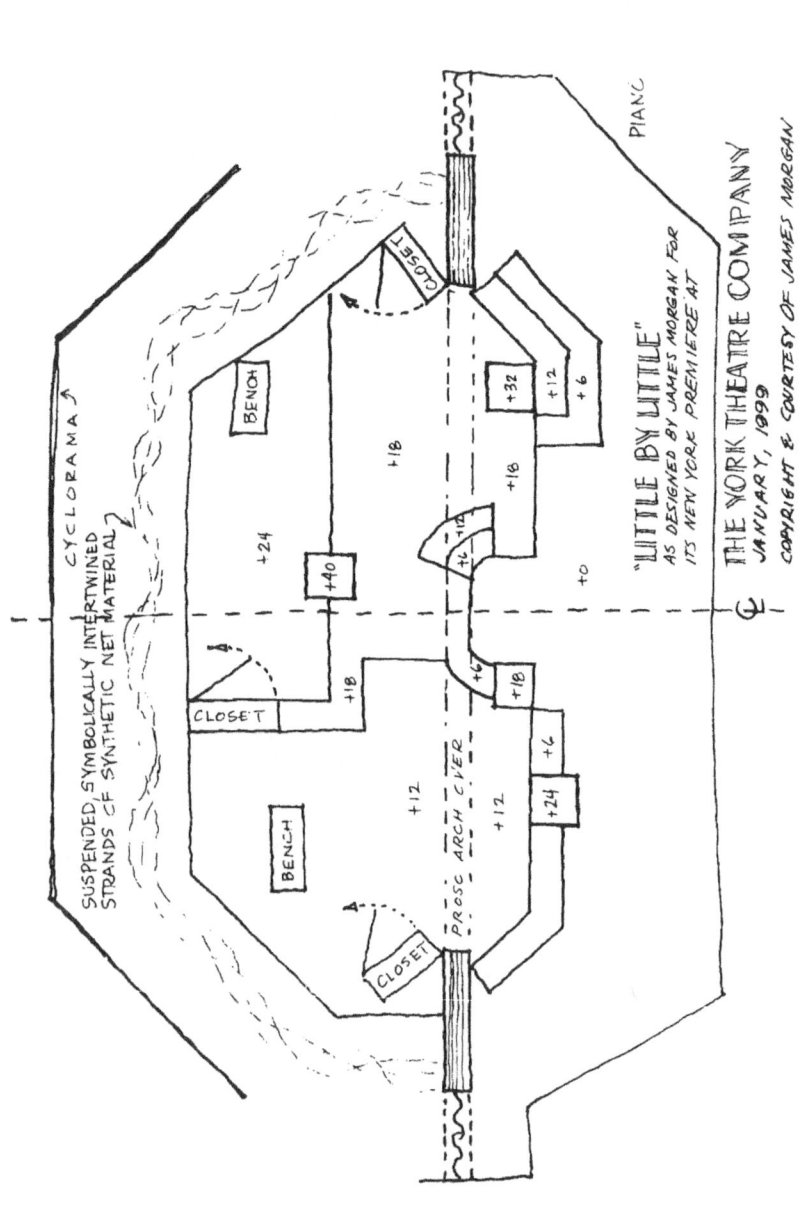

SUSPENDED, SYMBOLICALLY INTERTWINED
STRANDS OF SYNTHETIC NET MATERIAL

CYCLORAMA

BENCH

+24

+40

+18

+18

CLOSET

+18

BENCH

+12

+12

+12

+24

+6

+6

PROSC. ARCH. COVER

CLOSET

+6

+1/2

+18

+6

+1/2

+18

+0

+6

+12

+32

CLOSET

PIANO

"LITTLE BY LITTLE"
AS DESIGNED BY JAMES MORGAN FOR
ITS NEW YORK PREMIERE AT

THE YORK THEATRE COMPANY
JANUARY, 1999
COPYRIGHT & COURTESY OF JAMES MORGAN

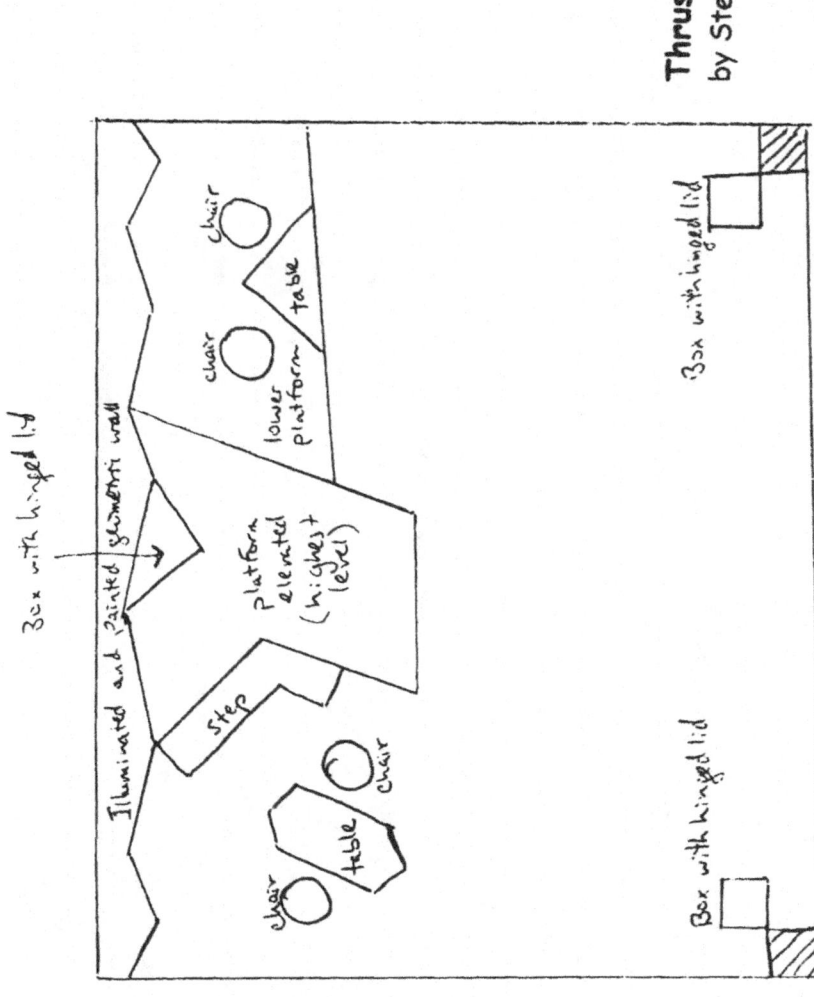

Thrust Stage Design
by Steve Lambert